MONSTAR
and the Haunted House

There are lots of Early Reader
stories you might enjoy.

Look at the back of the book or,
for a complete list, visit
www.orionchildrensbooks.co.uk

MONSTAR

and the Haunted House

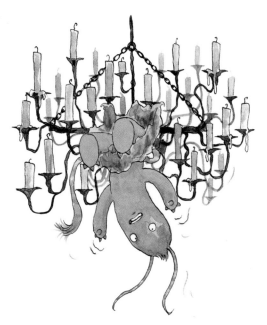

STEVE COLE
Illustrated by PETE WILLIAMSON

Orion
Children's Books

ORION CHILDREN'S BOOKS

First published in Great Britain in 2016
by Hodder and Stoughton

1 3 5 7 9 10 8 6 4 2

Text © Steve Cole, 2016
Illustrations © Pete Williamson, 2016

A CIP catalogue record for this book
is available from the British Library.

ISBN 978 1 4440 1467 9

Printed and bound in China

The paper and board used in this book are from well-managed forests
and other responsible sources.

MIX
Paper from
responsible sources
FSC® C104740

Orion Children's Books
An imprint of
Hachette Children's Group
Part of Hodder and Stoughton
Carmelite House
50 Victoria Embankment
London EC4Y 0DZ

An Hachette UK Company
www.hachette.co.uk

www.hachettechildrens.co.uk

To the Great Pumpkin

Contents

Chapter One

Jen and Jon had a special pet.
A big, green monster called
Monstar.

Monstar was a happy pet.
She loved her pink tutu, green
porridge and her family.

She did NOT love SCARY THINGS.

If Mum and Dad watched spooky films, Monstar hid under the chair.

If Jen told Jon a ghost story, Monstar hid under the bed.

So when Mum said, "We're all going to stay in a haunted house!" Monstar shivered so hard her furry knees knocked.

"Don't worry," said Jon. "We're only visiting Uncle Frankengrot."

"And cousin Honk," said Jen. "She's his daughter."

"Uncle Frankengrot is a mad scientist, like me and Mum," Dad explained. "Here is a photo of his house. What's scary about that?"

Monstar fainted.

Chapter Two

Monstar woke up just as the family arrived at a creepy castle.

"Hello!" Frankengrot came out, beaming. "Come in. Honk and I will show you round the house!"

Monstar gulped.

Inside, every room was dark and spooky and full of cobwebs.

One room was bigger than all the others. "This is my workshop," said Frankengrot.

Monstar saw there was something on the couch. Something very big and very bumpy and very, very lumpy.

"What's under the sheet?" Jen asked nervously.

Frankengrot smiled. "That's my top secret project."

"I bet it's horrid," said Honk.
"Everything's horrid in this horrid
old house."

She stomped off upstairs.

"Don't mind Honk," said
Frankengrot. "She is in a mood.
She wants us to move away and
live somewhere nice and normal."

Suddenly, everyone
heard a spooky noise.
"WOOOOOOOOOOOOOO!"

Monstar pointed to the doorway.

"It's… A GHOST!"

Chapter Three

Monstar tried to hide up Jon's jumper. It didn't work.

Then, as quickly as it had come, the ghost went away.

Seconds later, Honk ran in. "Did you see that ghost? It floated past me! Please, Father, can we move out and live somewhere nice?"

"There are no such things as ghosts," said Dad.

"We must have imagined it," said Frankengrot.

"Now, dinner is served in an hour. Honk and I will show you to your rooms so you can unpack."

Monstar had a room all to herself.
She didn't like it very much.

She decided to go downstairs to
the dining room to wait for dinner.

BUT…

The ghost was there!

Chapter Four

Monstar jumped so high in the air she got her tutu caught in the chandelier.

Jen and Jon and Mum and Dad and Frankengrot came running. But the ghost had gone.

"You imagined it, Monstar," said Mum.

"No! I saw the ghost too." Honk ran into the dining room. "This place is haunted. Please, let's move out!"

"A nice dinner will take your mind off it," said Frankengrot. "It's nearly ready. But first I must work some more on my secret project…"

He left, and Honk sighed. "I wish we lived somewhere pretty and nice."

Monstar licked her ear. "Me wish you did too!"

Chapter Five

After dinner, the grown-ups were boring and talked about inventions. Jen, Jon, Monstar and Honk went to bed.

"If you're scared, Monstar, you can sleep in our room," said Jon.

"You can build a den there," said Jen.

"WHEEEE!" Monstar licked them both. "Thank you."

She zoomed into her room and
pulled the covers off the bed.
Soon she had built a cosy nest on
the bedroom floor.

Monstar fell asleep. But she had funny dreams. She tossed and turned and wriggled and rolled in the bedsheets.

Then, Monstar was woken by a creak from the door – and a scream from Jon and Jen.

"Oh, no – it's the GHOST!"

Chapter Six

"EEEEK!" Monstar ran about in a panic. The sheets were over her head so she couldn't see anything.

WHUMP! She crashed into the ghost and fell down on top of it!

Now it was the ghost's turn to scream. "Help!" it said in a familiar voice. "Somebody get her off me!"

"That voice sounds familiar," said Jon.

Monstar finally pulled away her bedsheets – and found the 'ghost' was wearing sheets as well. Underneath . . . was Honk!

Mum, Dad and Frankengrot came rushing upstairs to investigate the screams.

"Monstar caught the ghost!" said Jen. "Except it wasn't a ghost – it was Honk all along!"

"Why are you pretending to be a ghost?" asked Frankengrot.

"I'm sorry," said Honk. "I just hate this spooky, dirty old house. I thought if I scared your visitors, you might agree to move somewhere nice."

"Oh, Honk!" Frankengrot hugged her. "I think you'd better meet my Secret Project."

"We've been helping him finish it,"
Dad explained.

"Come on!" said Mum.

Chapter Seven

Everyone ran down to the workshop. Monstar went first, feeling very brave and rather pleased with herself.

"Ta-daaa!" Frankengrot walked up
to the lumpy figure on the couch
and pulled away the blankets.

Underneath was a giant robot
holding a mop, a duster, paint and
a paintbrush!

The robot switched on.
"REDECORATE!" it said.
"CLEAN! TIDY!!"

"I know you want to live in a nice, clean house, Honk," said Frankengrot. "That's why I've built a decorating robot."

Mum laughed. "This house will be the smartest in town in no time!"

"It's brilliant!" Honk hugged her dad as the robot hoovered the hard to reach places. "Thank you!"

"And thank you, Monstar," said Jen. "You solved the mystery of the haunted house!"

"Three cheers for Monstar!"
Jon added.

But Monstar had already curled up on the floor and fallen asleep. Solving spooky mysteries was hard work – even for furry green monsters.